D1361099

SLED DOG DACHSHUND

by **LAURA ATKINS**

Illustrations by **An Phan**

**To my dog Milly,
who would give Jasper a run for his money.**

Traitor Dachshund, the children's imprint of Minted Prose, LLC
New York

www.traitordachshund.com

ISBN: 978-0-9965454-3-3

TRAITOR DACHSHUND® and ® are registered trademarks of Minted Prose, LLC

Printed in USA

10 9 8 7 6 5 4 3 2 1

SLED DOG DACHSHUND

by LAURA ATKINS

Illustrations by An Phan

TRAITOR DACHSHUND

NEW YORK

Jasper was snuggled in his cozy spot on the sofa when Dad peered over the newspaper. "There's a big sled race starting this weekend. It could be fun to go."

"Fantastic!" Jasper barked. "Can I be in it? I bet I could win!"

Dad laughed. "No, Jasper. You can't compete. This race is for the biggest and strongest dogs around. We'll just watch."

But Jasper's tail was already wagging
as he imagined himself running. His paws
hovered just over the finish line when—

"A dachshund could never win a big race like this,"
his big brother interrupted. "It takes around nine days.
Only big dogs can last that long."
Jasper didn't say anything.

A few days later, Jasper and his family wandered through the starting area of the race. They were way up north in Willow, Alaska, and the crisp air tickled their noses.

Jasper found a group of dogs lined up in front of a loaded sled.

"Where do I sign up?" he asked.

A husky grinned down at him. "You have to be part of a team," she said.

"A team?" Jasper cocked his head. He had never thought of being part of a team.

"Well, sure. It takes a whole group working together to win this race. I'm a lead dog," she said. "We set the pace and keep everyone on the trail."

"Great!" Jasper said. "I'll be a lead dog."

"You? You're too puny."

Before the lead dog knew it, Jasper had jumped into the harness.

His legs stuck out in every direction. The lead dog laughed.

Jasper moved farther down the line. "Can I race with you?" he asked.

The husky sniffed Jasper. "I'm a team dog. We need to keep up the pace that the lead dogs set. Can you do that?"

"Sure, I'm super fast," said Jasper. "Watch this."

He took off. And Jasper was fast . . .
until he hit a deep patch of snow.
The team dog chuckled.

Jasper trotted to the back of the pack where he found the biggest dog of all.

"What do you do on the team?" he asked.

"I'm a wheel dog. We're the first ones to get the heavy sled moving," the husky said.

"Let me try!" said Jasper.

The wheel dog lowered the harness so Jasper could get his feet on the ground.

The sled wouldn't budge.

The wheel dog laughed.

"You're not heavy enough."

Jasper was stumped.

"I need to be in the race!" he said.

Just then, the countdown started, and all of the dogs on the team turned their heads. Jasper saw his chance and dove into the sled.

Three . . . two . . . one . . .

They were **off!**

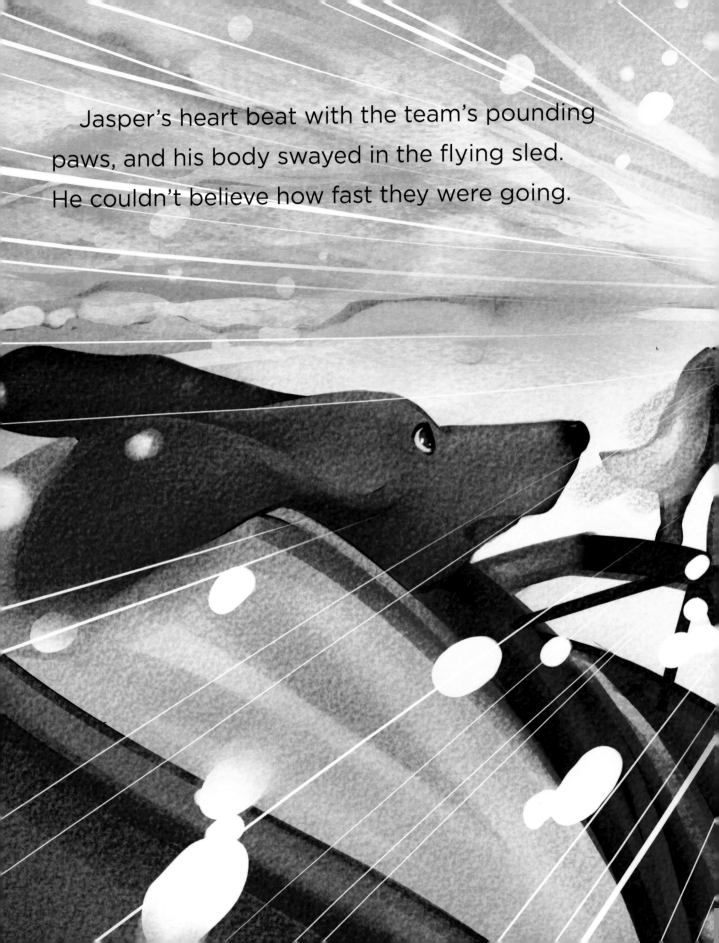

Jasper's heart beat with the team's pounding paws, and his body swayed in the flying sled. He couldn't believe how fast they were going.

But as the hours passed, Jasper noticed that
the barks of the lead dogs sounded weaker.
He peeked out.
The wheel dogs were straining.
The whole team was slowing down.
This is no way to win the race, Jasper thought.

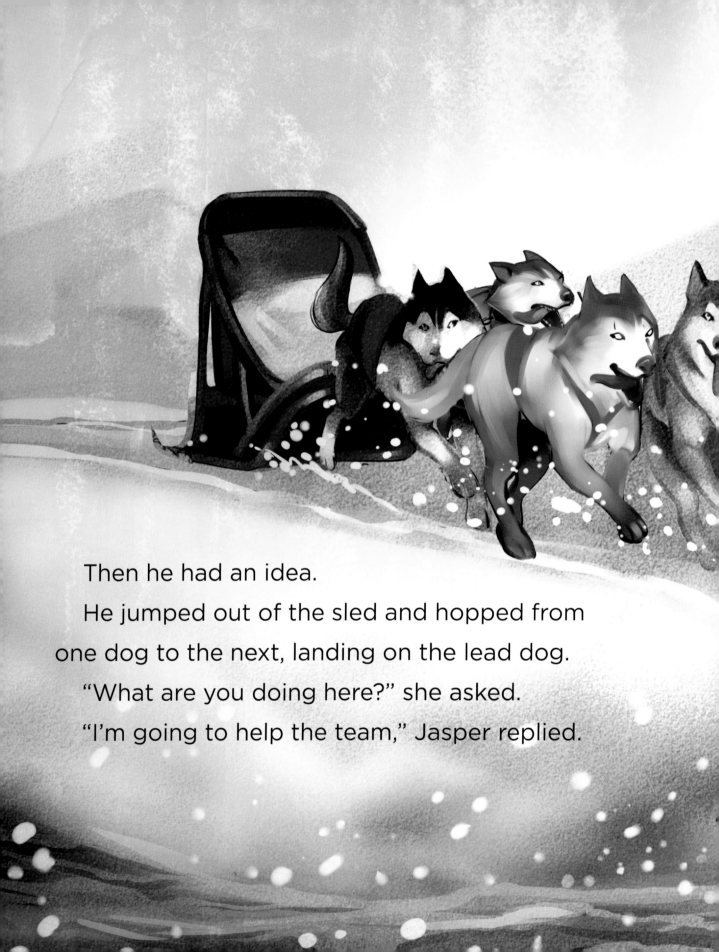

Then he had an idea.

He jumped out of the sled and hopped from one dog to the next, landing on the lead dog.

"What are you doing here?" she asked.

"I'm going to help the team," Jasper replied.

Then Jasper started to bark. His voice rang out in the cold air, and the dogs perked up their ears.

Their feet began striking the snow to the thumping rhythm of Jasper's barks.

They were back on track.

As the days went by, Jasper worked hard.

He snuggled up with the dogs during their short rest breaks because he was the world's best foot warmer.

When one of the lead dogs had a nightmare, Jasper sang a little tune, which settled her right down.

And always, when the dogs panted and dragged their paws as if they couldn't run another step, Jasper barked strong and loud. Everyone picked up the pace.

"This is great," Jasper said.

By the time the sun rose on the last morning
of the race, the team had charged into the lead.
As the dogs sprinted into the final stretch,
Jasper saw that they were giving it all they had.
But it wasn't enough.
Another sled pulled alongside them.

Jasper knew he could help.
He hopped to the lead dog to
bark out the pace. But he had
been barking for eight days,
and no sound came out.
Not even a yap.

The other team slipped ahead as
they approached the finish line.
This was it. He had to do something.

Jasper leaned forward,
stretching his hotdog body
as far as it could go . . .

The next thing he knew,
Jasper heard cheers all around.
His team had won the race.
And they had won it by
a nose—Jasper's nose.

Jasper jumped into a giant heap with his teammates.
The other dogs lifted him to the top of the pile.
"Three cheers for Sled Dog Dachshund,"
they barked.

Jasper had always known he could win. He had just needed the right team to do it.